A Socio-Mirror Story

Suparna Roy

Ukiyoto Publishing

All global publishing rights are held by

Ukiyoto Publishing

Published in 2025

Content Copyright © Suparna Roy

ISBN 9789367950319

All rights reserved.

No part of this publication may be reproduced, transmitted, or stored in a retrieval system, in any form by any means, electronic, mechanical, photocopying, recording or otherwise, without the prior permission of the publisher.

The moral rights of the author have been asserted.

This book is sold subject to the condition that it shall not by way of trade or otherwise, be lent, resold, hired out or otherwise circulated, without the publisher's prior consent, in any form of binding or cover other than that in which it is published.

www.ukiyoto.com

Exploring the Body-Stories!

The restroom on the third floor of the Hospital was a haven for me, a place I could lock out the world and steal a few moments of peace. The noise of the office was muffled behind the heavy door, and the cold, stark lighting offered no warmth but also no judgment. I leaned against the sink, looking at my reflection in the cracked mirror. My eyes were weary, and my uniform, though neatly pressed, felt like a shroud of exhaustion.

My name is Arpita Pal, and I work in the city's Emergency Response Unit (Health). For the past month, I'd been buried under a mountain of cases—everything from domestic disputes to violent crimes. It was my job to offer support and help, but the emotional toll was sometimes unbearable.

I splashed cold water on my face, hoping it would bring some clarity. There were few places I could truly call my own in the chaos of my daily life. The restroom, though small and unremarkable, was one such place. It was my sanctuary, where I could momentarily escape the world's demands.

As I dried my hands, the sharp ring of my phone jolted me back to reality. I glanced at the screen. It was a message from my partner, Mark: "We need to talk. ASAP."

A sinking feeling settled in my stomach. Mark and I had been working together for years, and his terse messages usually meant something serious was up. I stepped out of the restroom and made my way to his office, trying to ignore the unease gnawing at me.

Mark's office was a small, cluttered space filled with case files and old coffee cups. He was hunched over his desk, his face obscured by shadows from the desk lamp. The lines of stress were etched deeply into his features. He looked up as I entered his expression unreadable.

"Sit down," he said, gesturing to the chair opposite him.

I sat, my heart pounding. "What's going on?"

Mark's eyes met mine, and for a moment, he seemed to struggle with what to say. Finally, he took a deep breath and spoke. "We've got a new case. It's… it's a tough one."

I leaned forward, my curiosity piqued. "What's the details?"

Mark hesitated before sliding a file across the desk to me. "It's a rape case. The victim, Abhaya, is one of our own. She's an intern with the city's doctoral unit program."

My stomach churned. Abhaya was someone I knew, if only in passing. She was always kind and composed someone who seemed to have a natural ability to help others. The thought of her being a victim was almost incomprehensible.

Mark continued, "Abhaya was attacked last night. She's in the hospital, and she's not talking much. The case is complicated, and I need you to be the lead investigator. I know you're already stretched thin, but—"

"I'll do it," I interrupted, my voice steady despite the turmoil inside me. "Where is she?"

Mark provided the hospital details, and I left his office, my mind racing. The day had taken a turn I hadn't anticipated, and the weight of the task ahead felt almost unbearable.

The hospital (where Abhaya was admitted) was quiet when I arrived, a stark contrast to the chaos of the working space. I navigated the sterile corridors, my footsteps echoing in the emptiness. Jenna's room was on the second floor, and I took the elevator up, trying to steal myself for what I might find.

When I entered her room, Abhaya was lying in bed, her face pale and drawn. The bruises and swelling were visible even through the thin hospital gown. The body of the victim, a young woman, was discovered in a secluded, abandoned. The victim's body was found in a state of severe decomposition, indicating that she had mentally been deceased for several days. The forensic team and police quickly secured the scene, collecting crucial evidence and documenting the condition of the body. She looked up as I approached, her eyes filled with a mixture of fear and resignation.

"Abhaya," I said softly, taking a seat beside her bed. "I'm Arpita. I'm here to help."

Her gaze flickered with something akin to hope, though it was quickly overshadowed by a deep sadness. She didn't speak, merely nodded. I could see the strain in her eyes, the weight of her trauma too heavy for words.

"I know it's hard," I continued gently. "But if you can tell me what happened, it will help us find the person responsible. We want to make sure this doesn't happen to anyone else."

Abaya's eyes filled with tears, and she took a shuddering breath. "I was… I was leaving work late. I often stay behind to finish up reports. Last night, I stayed even later. I don't know why, but something felt... off."

Her voice broke, and she paused, struggling to continue. I reached out and took her hand, offering a comforting squeeze. "It's okay. Take your time."

She nodded, her tears falling freely now. "I was in the parking lot. I heard footsteps behind me, but I didn't think anything of it. Then... then someone grabbed me from behind. I tried to scream, but he... he covered my mouth. He forced me into the alley behind the building. I... I couldn't fight back. I felt so powerless."

Her words were like daggers, each one cutting deeper into my heart. I could see the pain etched in her features, the memories replaying in her mind. It was all too familiar—too many victims had shared similar stories, and each one was a stark reminder of the brutality that existed in the world.

"Did you see his face?" I asked softly, trying to guide the conversation gently.

Abhaya shook her head, her expression one of deep regret. "No. He was wearing a hood. I couldn't see his face, only his eyes. They were cold—cold and unfeeling."

I nodded, taking notes as she spoke. The information was crucial, but it was clear that Abhaya's pain was far from over. I promised her that we would do everything in our power to find the person responsible and left her room with a heavy heart.

As I walked back through the hospital's corridors, I felt a profound sense of responsibility settle over me. Jenna's case was now my focus, and I was determined to see it through. I would need to gather evidence, interview witnesses, and piece together the fragments of Jenna's story to find the perpetrator.

The investigation was grueling. I interviewed Abhaya's colleagues and reviewed security footage from the building. I spoke with witnesses who had been in the area that night, piecing together a timeline of events. Each step forward was painstaking, and the emotional toll was immense.

After days of relentless work, we had a breakthrough. One of the security cameras had captured a figure matching the description Abhaya had provided. The footage was grainy, but it was enough to identify a suspect—a man with a history of violent offenses. His name was Saikat Ghosh, a doctor.

We brought Ghosh in for questioning, and he initially denied any involvement. But under the pressure of the evidence and the weight of his own guilt, he eventually confessed. He had been lurking around the area, waiting for an opportunity. When he saw Abhaya alone, he seized his chance.

The trial that followed was a long and arduous process. Abhaya testified bravely, her courage inspiring everyone who witnessed her strength. Ghosh was convicted, and the verdict brought a measure of justice, though it could never fully undo the harm he had caused.

Abhaya eventually returned to her work, though she struggled with the scars left by the trauma. I kept in touch with her, offering support and ensuring she had access to the help she needed. Her strength and resilience became a beacon for others who had suffered similar experiences.

Eventually, an unnamed story writer emailed me during this case was going on…I still remember how suddenly an emailed popped up my screen stating a 'Hi'. What pinched me to reply back was the name which 'unnamed sr'. As I started the conversation, this person asked me, "Can I write a story on the current case that you are investigating, which may help you get closer to the justice and amplify the message?"

I thought for a while and then immediately went to Abhaya if she was comfortable with this process. When I went to meet her, I saw her reading a story named "The Girl". When I asked her would she be fine if this happens and showed her all my conversation with this 'unnamed sr'. Abhaya's silence made me felt foolish, so I apologized and started back when she called me and said, she would not only love to see this published but also exactly the way it took place, so that she can become a surviving example of strength. I hugged her and left.

I emailed this writer and asked her to come over a café to move ahead. I asked her to meet me the very next day a Maya Café and made the script overnight to hand it to her. I do not know what was driving me to do it so immensely. I met the 'unnamed sr' in Maya Café, and handed her the script.

It was in the Scripted Magazine of Protest that a month later I read this title- Abhaya, which showcased-

Abhaya sat in the sterile hospital room, the soft hum of the fluorescent lights above mingling with the beeping of the heart monitor beside her bed. The room was devoid of personal touches—no photographs, no flowers, only the pale green walls and the stark, clinical furniture. Her mind was a whirl of confusion and pain, making it hard to focus on anything beyond the immediate discomfort of the hospital bed and the bruising soreness that seemed to permeate every inch of her body.

Her thoughts kept spiraling back to the events of the previous night. She had been finishing up some reports at her office, the quiet hum of the air conditioning the only sound apart from the occasional clatter of her keyboard. She had been working late, as she often did, and as she left the building, the cold night air had felt like a thin veil over the city's relentless pace. That was when he had appeared—a figure emerging from the darkness, his presence so abrupt and sinister that she had been paralyzed with fear. Everything after that had become a blur of pain and terror.

As she tried to piece together the fragments of her shattered night, there was a soft knock on the door, and it opened slowly. In walked Arpita, an investigator from the local police department. Arpita was a woman of average height, with a calm and composed demeanor that contrasted sharply with the chaos Abhaya felt inside. Her dark hair was pulled back in a neat ponytail, and she wore a crisp, navy-blue suit that spoke of professionalism and authority. She carried a leather briefcase, which she set down gently beside a chair before taking a seat.

"Hello, Abhaya," Arpita said, her voice calm and soothing. "My name is Arpita, and I'm the investigator assigned to your case. I'm here to speak with you about what happened. I know this is a difficult time, and I want to assure you that I'm here to help."

Abhaya managed a small nod, her throat tight and dry. She had been dreading this moment, the moment when she would have to relive her nightmare for someone else. Her eyes met Arpita's, and she could see genuine concern and empathy in them. It was a small comfort amidst the sea of overwhelming emotions.

Arpita began by asking Abhaya if she felt ready to talk, emphasizing that she could take things at her own pace. Abhaya took a deep breath, trying to steady her trembling hands. "I—I'll try," she said, her voice barely above a whisper.

Arpita opened her briefcase and took out a notepad and pen, ready to take down any information that Abhaya was comfortable sharing. "Whenever you're ready, just start from the beginning. Anything you can tell me will help."

Abhaya's mind flashed back to the night before. She closed her eyes briefly, trying to push aside the wave of nausea that threatened to overtake her. "I was at the office," she began, her voice shaky. "I was finishing some reports. It was late, but I often stay behind to get work done. I was leaving around midnight. I felt... uneasy, like someone was watching me, but I didn't see anyone."

Arpita nodded encouragingly, her expression one of patience and understanding. "Did you notice anything unusual? Anything at all that seemed out of place?"

Abhaya's mind struggled to focus. "No, not really. I just felt... uncomfortable. When I walked to my car, I heard footsteps behind me, but I didn't turn around. I thought it was just my imagination. Then, he was there."

Her voice faltered, and she paused, the memory of the attack flooding her senses. Arpita leaned forward slightly, her gaze gentle but intent. "It's okay. Take your time."

Abhaya took a deep breath, her chest tight. "He grabbed me from behind. He covered my mouth with something, maybe a cloth. I couldn't scream. I tried to fight him off, but he was so strong. He dragged me to an alley behind the building. I was so scared. I kept thinking, 'This can't be happening.'"

Tears streamed down Abhaya's face, and she wiped them away with the back of her hand. Arpita's gaze remained steady, her demeanor unflinching. "You're doing very well," she said softly. "Was there anything about him that you remember clearly? Any details that stood out?"

Abhaya's memory was a haze of fear and pain. "He was wearing a hood, so I couldn't see his face. His eyes were cold—just empty. He didn't say much, just grunted. I remember feeling so helpless, like I was trapped in a nightmare."

Arpita scribbled notes quickly, her pen moving efficiently across the page. "We'll use that description to try and identify him. Did you notice any specific features or anything he said that might help us?"

Abhaya shook her head slowly. "No, he didn't talk much. I couldn't see his face clearly. He was rough, and I felt like I was just... an object to him. When he was done, he just left me there. I don't know how long I was lying there before someone found me."

Arpita's face remained a mask of professional empathy. "Thank you for sharing that with me. I know it's incredibly difficult to relive these moments, and your bravery is important in helping us pursue this case."

Abhaya nodded, feeling a mixture of relief and exhaustion. The conversation had taken a toll on her, but there was also a small flicker of hope that justice might be within reach. Arpita continued to ask questions about the immediate aftermath, the medical examination, and the support services available to Abhaya. She handed over brochures and contact information for counseling services and support groups, emphasizing that Abhaya was not alone and had a network of people ready to help her.

As the meeting drew to a close, Arpita stood up, preparing to leave. She looked at Abhaya with a mixture of respect and concern. "Thank you again for your courage today, Abhaya. We will use all the information you've provided to further the investigation and seek justice. If you need anything or have any more information, don't hesitate to reach out."

Abhaya managed a weak smile, her emotions a turbulent mix of sadness and gratitude. "Thank you, Arpita. It helps to know that someone cares and is working to find him."

Arpita gave her a reassuring nod before leaving the room, her mind already turning over the details of the case and the steps needed to advance the investigation. The encounter had been emotionally draining but necessary. Arpita knew that the path to justice would be long and arduous, but she was committed to pursuing it with diligence and compassion.

For Abhaya, the meeting with Arpita was a moment of both vulnerability and strength. It was a difficult step toward confronting the trauma she had endured, but it also provided her with a sense of hope and reassurance. The professional and empathetic approach of the investigator offered Abhaya a glimmer of faith that the justice she sought was possible, and that her voice would not be lost in the struggle for accountability.

After thoroughly reading the story the 'unnamed sr' wrote in the magazine, I felt as if this person somewhere echoed the entire experience through her pen, although with some minor changes. I wanted to talk to this writer once again, and know more about *her*.

I emailed the writer and asked her to meet me at the same Maya Café, once again. The case of Abhaya at the end was resolved but the impact remained through every nerve that I faced. The internet was flooded with this story by 'unnamed sr' and kept with their protest on until the accused was finally sentenced to life imprisonment. My own experience of working on the case changed me profoundly. I was more aware than ever of the struggles faced by survivors and the importance of offering genuine support and understanding.

Meeting the 'unnamed sr' after a month and between all these protests gave a different vibe. She acme and sat in front me; her hairs mantled with tiredness, gave me an expression of a suppressed spirit. I formally began the conversation asking, "How are you?", and also added "Thanks" for making this investigation beautifully penned into protest fire. I also added that had it not been for her initiative to write a story on this, the case would never get such support and prudent justice. Hearing my blabbering, she only nodded. I, then asked her, "what made you contact me suddenly and what motivated you to write this incident as a story?"

I will never forget the way she looked at me hearing this question… I thought I was mistaken somewhere, so to get the tone back, I apologized. She, then, looked at then looked at the window, shook her head, gasped a deep breath and said, "Silence does not Suit Women." She then said, her name was Sumita Rai (sr), and she, too, was a victim of this Saikat Ghosh years ago. Listening to this, I was flabbergasted. She, then started how and why did this happen to her.

It was back in 2022, that she took an appointment to diagnose herself to this Dr. Saikat Ghosh. She was a resident of the community this Doctor used to stay. This figure was respected beyond measure in her society. She said, "Since childhood, I am an introvert person, I hardly shared my experience with anyone, and was always silent of my sufferings."

She then, again began…

I was in his private home chamber alongside 8 other patients. Never more than ten patients were allowed in his private chamber which is organized in his house. I and my family were known to him. I was the last one. I waited almost for thirty minutes and then began the most terrible forty-five minutes of my life. He was a Neurologist, and I went to him to get redressed of my migraine which was then a very common visitor to my life; in fact, one day I fainted in middle of my work. So, with urgency only, I made this attempt to get a treatment of it. I still remember, as soon I entered his cabin, he asked me to sit and narrate my problem, and like an obedient patient I unfolded myself to him. He got up and came near me and asked me to relax, holding my head in his hand he eventually pressed different areas on my scalp asking where do get immense pain. The process made me felt a bit uncomfortable, but I thought maybe this was okay! Eventually his hands went through my neck and started messaging... I got afraid, I left my seat and stood up asking his leave... it was when he suddenly pulled me holding my waist and pushed me in the chair, groped my chin and said- "You are alone here, I will kill you if any noise is done, sit and listen." I was cold and pale, silent and disabled... unable to speak; I almost shivered when I felt his hands on my breasts, crushing them like sponge balls. I made hurting sound, when he threw water in my face asking me to keep silent... afraid, I did as he said, and with each passing moment I felt dirty and disgusted... his hands from my breasts went to my nipples pulling them hard and making me cry harder. When he found no sense of pleasure in my body, he took out his penis and started masturbating. I kept silent and he asked me to open my clothes, shouted and threw water on my chest. When I refrained from opening my clothes, he tore apart my Kurti and bra… when I started to run to save my body, he slapped me and pushed me hard against the wall, and I fainted. The next morning I found myself in the verandah of my home, covered in white clothes with this monster sitting in front of me and my parents.

I kept shouting and saying my parents that Saikat sir molested me, but my parents were brainwashed with a different narrative by that monster; wherein, he found me in this horrific condition in the road, and brought me here hiddenly in his car, and this being early morning no one would doubt what happened and my family's prestige would be untouched. He clearly gave an open warning to my parents to remain quiet and he will try providing me with financial help and find a suitable boy. I cried, shouted, blamed, but all in vain. I said my parents everything I remember before fainting, but they only asked me to remain quiet for the family's sake and prestige.

Sumita looked at me, ad said- "This shame kills uncountable girls' everyday!"

18   A Socio-Mirror Story

Sumita continued, and said… I tried walking but my legs were still shivering, and after hours I got up, took bath and gathered all possible courage and went to the chamber and said loudly in front of his assistant and patients what he did with me! I was forcibly pushed out and sent back, coming home, I found my father paralyzed, and my mother blamed me saying "Why could you not keep shut… taking your father's life will give you peace." Immediately I received a call from n unknown number which when I responded warned mildly that, "This time is just paralyzed…next time you open your mouth, you father will be killed and mother will face the same condition you faced." Since then, I remained quiet and restored to silence.

I kept quiet, and observed the tears that flowed through Sumita's eyes. I was shattered and could say nothing. Sumit, then said that when this investigation of Abhaya's case was getting rumored; she felt something must be done and so decided to help us only with a hope to gave punishment to this monstrous clothed Doctor. Sumita said that she would now have to leave, for the timing of a physiotherapist to visit her father is nearing. I could say nothing, still, I remained silent. I just hugged her with a hope to take way all her pain; unfortunately, which I couldn't!

The restroom on the third floor of the Hospital, once a sanctuary of solitude, had become a place where I confronted my own limitations and found the resolve to face the harsh realities of my work. Abhaya's and Sumita's case reminded me of the profound responsibility we have in seeking justice and offering support to those in need.

It was a long, difficult journey, but through it all, I learned that even in the darkest of times, there is hope—and the strength to face what comes next made me realize that this was more than just a discovery—it was a beginning. The answers I sought, the mysteries that had eluded me, were all within reach. This realm held the potential to change everything I thought I knew about the world.

With renewed purpose, I stepped forward, ready to embrace the unknown and uncover the secrets of this extraordinary place called 'body'.

About the Author

Suparna Roy

Suparna Roy is an Assistant Professor of English (Dept of Applied Sciences and Humanities) at Global Institute of Management and Technology, and an Independent Researcher. She has qualified CTET and has obtained her Master's in English Literature (2020) and completed her B. ED in 2022.

Besides her academic qualifications, she has a first-class in French intermediate language learning (2019), and experience teaching for more than three years in various fields. She is deeply engaged in the research of South Asian studies focusing on Gender and Literature from an intersectional perspective.

She has more than 20 publications (journals, chapters in books, pre-prints, magazines, e-newspaper, book), and 30+ presentations until that date. She has also completed one research project on Queer Identities and Gender Intersectionality; one under Think India Tribal Rights Forum. She was also selected for Doctoral Research Program under Summer Sexuality Fellowship 2022 at California Institute of Integrated Studies (*https://professorpennyharvey.weebly.com/ciis-sexuality-summer-research-fellowship.*) under Dr. Penny Harvey and Dr. Michelle Marzullo. She is also a selected researcher in the En-gender group- *https://engenderacademia.wordpress.com/south-asian-studies/*.

www.ingramcontent.com/pod-product-compliance
Lightning Source LLC
LaVergne TN
LVHW041603070526
838199LV00047B/2120